Here

I Can Be Mindful

by Ally Condie

illustrated by Jaime Kim

VIKING

Some days the world is a warm gold sun.
Some days it is a green grass wave.

Some days it is a bright blue ball.

Some days it is a cool gray stone.

Some days, some hours, some minutes
are good.

Some days, some hours, some minutes
are hard.

Today I am here.

Feeling sad.
Feeling worried.
Feeling frustrated.
Feeling lonely.

But I know
there are ways to help.

I hold them in my hand.

Like a marble,
an acorn,

a leaf,
a feather.

Here.

When I am worried,
I remember—

Feel.

A leaf in my fingers.
My feet on the ground.

Taste.

A crisp apple.
A warm cookie.

Look.
Close.

So close.

Hear.

The wind. Sing to trees.
A breath, in and out.

Smell.
Rainy sidewalk.
Night air.

Say.
Here I am in my body.
Here I am in the world.

Run.
So hard.
So fast.

Jump.
And jump and
jump and jump.

Draw. Write.
Tell the words how I feel.
Tell the colors what to say.

Go.
Someplace f a r a w a y.

Or someplace very close.

Tell.
Someone how I am feeling.

I need a hug.
I need a back scratch.

I need you not to touch me.
I need you to hold me very tight.

Do.
Something for
someone else.

for
mom

Think.

I am grateful for . . .

Remember.
Lots of people love me.

Know
I am

Here.

For Truman,
I am so glad you are here. —A. C.

For Henry —J. K.

VIKING
An imprint of Penguin Random House LLC, New York

First published in the United States of America by Viking, an imprint of Penguin Random House LLC, 2023

Text copyright © 2023 by Allyson Braithwaite Condie
Illustrations copyright © 2023 by Jaime Kim

Visit us online at penguinrandomhouse.com.

Library of Congress Cataloging-in-Publication Data is available.

Manufactured in China

ISBN 9780593327142

1 3 5 7 9 10 8 6 4 2

TOPL

Design by Kate Renner
Text set in Farthing and Grobek Alt

The art for this book was made using digital tools.